Pout-Pout Fish
Haunted House

Written by **Wes Adams**   Illustrated by **Isidre Monés**

Based on the *New York Times*–bestselling Pout-Pout Fish books
written by Deborah Diesen and illustrated by Dan Hanna

SCHOLASTIC INC.

D0753754

ISBN 978-1-338-61133-5

12 11 10 9 8 7 6 5 4   19 20 21 22 23 24

Printed in the U.S.A.   40

First Scholastic printing, September 2019

Designed by Aram Kim

Mr. Fish was nervous about going out on Halloween. He didn't like getting spooked, but he loved costumes and candy.

He was meeting his friend from the deep sea, Mr. Lantern.
Together, they were going to explore
Miss Shimmer's haunted house.

"BOO!" said Mr. Lantern.
"Boo to you!" said Mr. Fish.
He was happy not to be alone.

All sorts of frightful creatures were trick-or-treating. Mr. Fish got scared.

"Keep up!" said Mr. Lantern. "Don't be fooled by make-believe monsters."

Mr. Fish felt a little better as he joined the crowd.

But his worries came rushing back when he and his friend approached the haunted house. "Just remember, it's only pretend," said Mr. Lantern.

They came to an entrance
guarded by a shark—
or was it a sea turtle?

"Enter, if you dare," the gatekeeper said.
Down a passage the two visitors swam.
Pout-Pout Fish shivered when they came
to a gloomy room filled with ghosts.

"Relax," whispered Mr. Lantern. "They're not real."
Mr. Fish saw that the glowing creatures were just
jellyfish floating happily this way and that.

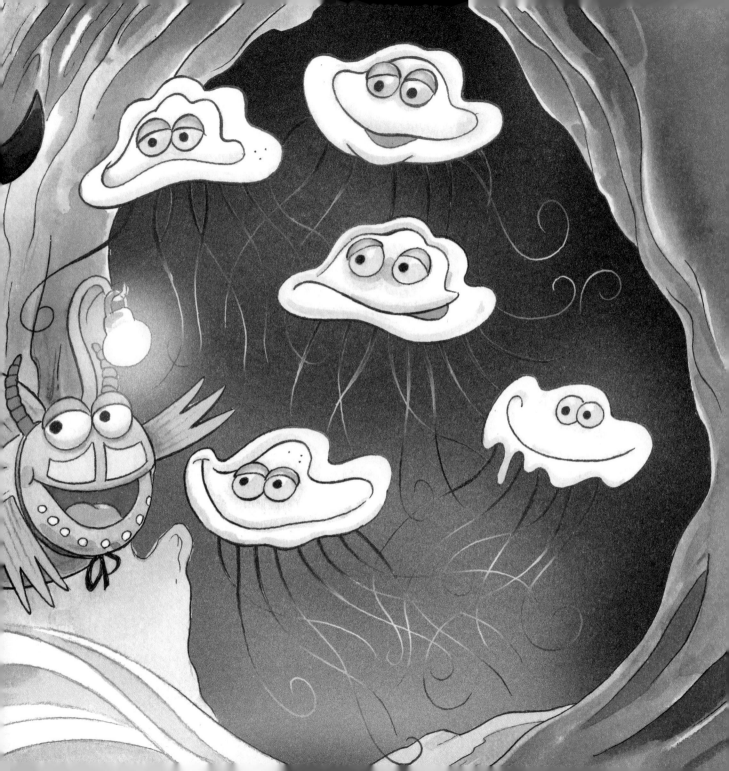

Mr. Lantern led the way to
another dark space. By the shock of
light from an eerie electric eel,
Mr. Fish saw creepy-crawlies
everywhere.

"Don't fret," said his friend.

Mr. Lantern's globe lit up the scene, and the eel disappeared. Mr. Fish saw that it was only a lobster and two crabs.

He told himself to be brave as he and Mr. Lantern swam away—straight toward another scary surprise!

This time, Mr. Lantern almost fainted from fright, but Pout-Pout Fish wasn't fooled. "Hello, Mr. Eight!" he greeted his octopus friend, whose tentacles were decorated to look like snakes.

"We've been waiting for you," said Mr. Eight. He pointed to a seaweed-covered doorway.

Inside, a party was underway. There were treats, games, music, and dancing. Miss Shimmer smiled when she saw that Mr. Fish and Mr. Lantern had arrived.

"HAPPY HALLOWEEN!" Pout-Pout Fish said to all his friends as he swam inside to join the fright-filled fun.

Jeremy   1995

Merry Christmas

Love,

Harold

SIERRA CLUB
WILDLIFE
LIBRARY

SNAKES

SIERRA CLUB WILDLIFE LIBRARY SNAKES

Eric S. Grace

General Editor, R. D. Lawrence

Sierra Club Books for Children
San Francisco

The Sierra Club, founded in 1892 by John Muir, has devoted itself to the study and protection of the earth's scenic and ecological resources – mountains, wetlands, woodlands, wild shores and rivers, deserts and plains. The publishing program of the Sierra Club offers books to the public as a nonprofit educational service in the hope that they may enlarge the public's understanding of the Club's basic concerns. The Sierra Club has some sixty chapters in the United States and in Canada. For information about how you may participate in its programs to preserve wilderness and the quality of life, please address inquiries to Sierra Club, 730 Polk Street, San Francisco, CA 94109.

First edition

Photographs: © D. G. Barker / Tom Stack, 1, 53; © J. Cancalosi / Tom Stack, 26, 35, 36; © Comstock, 43; © David M. Dennis / Tom Stack, 21, 54; © D. Fernandez & M. Peck, 27, 48, 57; © Kerry T. Givens / Tom Stack, 10; © Nick Greaves / Planet Earth, 6, 44, 49; © Ken Lucas / Planet Earth, 33, 42, 58; © Roy Luckow, 22; © Wayne Lynch, 3, 5, 9, 14, 23, 29; © Robert McCaw, 7, 16; © Joe McDonald / Tom Stack, 25, 34, 40; © Richard Matthews / Planet Earth, 31; © Mark Mattock / Planet Earth, 17; © F. C. Millington / Planet Earth, 11; © Brian Milne / First Light, 61; © R. W. Murphy, 37; © George Peck, 38; © E. Hanumantha Rao / WWF, 32; © Peter Velensky / Planet Earth, 46; © G. Wiltsie / First Light, 52; © Robert Zakrison, 20.

Library of Congress Cataloging-in-Publication Data

Grace, Eric S.
　　Snakes / Eric S. Grace; general editor, R.D. Lawrence.
　　　　p.　　cm – (Sierra Club wildlife library)
　　Includes index.
　　ISBN 0-87156-490-4
　　1. Snakes – Juvenile literature.　[1. Snakes.]　I. Lawrence, R.D.,
1921-　.　II. Title.　III. Series.
QL666.O6G68　1994
597.96 – dc20　　　　　　　　　　　　　　　　　93-45407

Published in Canada by Key Porter Books Limited

Printed in China

10 9 8 7 6 5 4 3 2 1

Contents

Slithering Serpents   6

Cold-Blooded Reptiles   9

Snake Anatomy   14

Snake Families   27

The Hunt for Food   43

Snake Reproduction   52

Snakes in Their Environment   57

Index   63

Slithering Serpents

The African python can grow to twenty feet long. It is not poisonous but kills its prey by constriction.

The first time I had the chance to handle a big snake, I was thrilled. I was ten years old and visiting a zoo with my school class. The keeper took an African python out of its cage and asked, "Anyone want to hold it?" I thought everyone would leap at the chance, so I was a little puzzled to find myself first in a line of one. The snake was probably no more than five feet long, although it looked bigger to us children. It was heavy and felt warm and dry. Its red tongue flicked in and out as it glided slowly up my arm and across my shoulder. I felt the powerful grip of its solid body and wondered for a brief moment if it would wrap itself around my neck and strangle me.

I soon discovered that many people are afraid of snakes. They don't like to get close to even the most harmless and beautiful of these animals. Is it because snakes look so different from us? Is it because they appear secretive and dangerous?

Actually, snakes *are* secretive, and with good reason. Life close to the ground is full of danger. And snakes cannot move nearly as fast as similar-size animals with legs. Because of this, they usually take good care to stay out of our way.

But are they dangerous? Most of them aren't. More than 75 percent of the world's snakes are not poisonous and are no threat to people. Of the few hundred types of poisonous snakes in the world, only about half can kill people – and most of those live in tropical countries. In North America, more people are killed each year by bee stings than by snakebites.

Of course, it's a good idea to be cautious when approaching any wild animal. But the more you learn about snakes, the less you will fear them and the more you will come to admire their remarkable ways of life.

Garter snakes are the
most common snakes in
North America.

Snakes are found in every part of the world except the Antarctic and the tops of high mountain ranges. Snakes live in forests, in fields and grasslands, in city parks and gardens, in some of the driest deserts on Earth, in swamps and ponds, and in the oceans.

There is nearly as much variety among snakes as there is among birds. There are burrowing snakes that eat worms, and water snakes that catch fish. There are snakes that can glide from tree to tree. There are snakes that hunt by day, and others that hunt at night. There are snakes small enough to fit in the palm of your hand, and snakes so big they can stretch all the way from the ground to the roof of a three-story house.

Despite such differences, all snakes have some things in common – the things that make them snakes and not some other kind of animal. For example, all snakes are covered with scales, and they move easily and gracefully without arms, legs, fins, or wings. Snakes also have special senses. They can hear with their lungs and smell with their tongues.

Around the house where I live now, I often see garter snakes in the summer when I am gardening or walking my dog. I always stop to look at them and imagine what they were doing just before I discovered them. Was this snake on its way to find a meal? Was it looking for a mate? Or had it come out into the open to bask in the sun? I watch the snake's sides move in and out with each breath. I wonder what it makes of me, a large shape squatting down beside it. The more we learn about the lives of other animals, even such strange-seeming animals as snakes, the more we come to understand the important roles they play in the community of all living things.

Cold-Blooded Reptiles

What sort of animals are snakes? Like us, snakes have bony skeletons, brains, hearts, and lungs, and they breathe air. Unlike us, they have scaly skins and are cold-blooded. That means their body temperature depends mostly on the temperature of their surroundings (see page 11). Snakes are part of a larger group of animals called reptiles, which also includes lizards, crocodiles, alligators, turtles, and a lizardlike animal called a tuatara.

Crocodiles, like snakes, are reptiles.

About six thousand different species of reptiles are living today, nearly half of which are snakes. But many other sorts of reptiles lived on Earth in the past. The most famous of these ancient reptiles are the dinosaurs, which first appeared just over 225 million years ago. The long period that began then is sometimes called the Age of Reptiles. During this period, dinosaurs lived in swamps, deserts, and forests around the world. Flying reptiles soared through the air, and whale-size reptiles hunted in lakes and oceans. Nearly all of these reptiles became extinct more than 65 million years ago. We know about them today only from some of their remains that were preserved as fossils.

Two important things helped reptiles become such a widespread group of animals for such a long time: their scaly skins and their eggs. To understand why these are important, compare reptiles with amphibians, such as frogs and newts.

Amphibians are a group of animals that evolved to live on land before reptiles did. Most amphibians have thin skin that easily dries out in the air. They usually lay their eggs in jellylike clusters in streams or ponds or under rotting logs. Because their thin skins and their eggs need to stay moist, most amphibians cannot live long far from water or damp soil.

Reptiles are better prepared to avoid dehydration

9

A rough green snake protects the eggs it has laid.

than amphibians are. A reptile's scaly skin is waterproof, keeping its body from drying out. Most reptile eggs are large and yolky with leathery shells that help prevent them from losing moisture. Thanks to their scaly skins and large, tough-shelled eggs, reptiles can live in many different places on land far from water. Reptiles are at home in dry deserts and grasslands where most amphibians could not survive.

Some reptiles, including many snakes, go one step further to protect their eggs from a harsh, dry environment. They do not lay eggs at all; instead, they keep the eggs inside their bodies until the young have completely developed. These reptiles give birth to live young.

Snakes first appeared on Earth more recently than other reptiles. The oldest fossils of snakes are only about 135 million years old. Snakes probably evolved from burrowing lizards, which did not need legs for moving through narrow tunnels in the ground. Several burrowing lizards living today, such as skinks, have very short legs and long, snakelike bodies. One species of lizard – the slow worm – has no legs at all. At first sight, these legless lizards look much like snakes, but there are a few important differences between the two types of reptiles (see the box on page 12).

One bit of evidence that snakes' ancestors had legs is found inside the bodies of some snakes such as boas and pythons. The skeletons of these snakes have a small pelvis and tiny rear leg bones. In some species, the leg bones end in small claws, called *spurs*, which stick out from the snake's body near the base of its tail.

If you've ever seen snakes in a zoo, you've probably noticed that they don't move much. They seem content to spend all day lying still. Part of the reason for this is the way snakes – and other reptiles – respond to the temperature of their surroundings.

Most animals need to have their bodies at a certain temperature for them to work efficiently. For instance, the normal human body temperature is usually 98.6°F (37°C). Your body temperature doesn't go much above or below this unless you are sick with a fever or a severe chill. In warm-blooded mammals and birds, body temperature is controlled from the inside. The muscles of these animals burn energy and make heat. Their fat and fur or feathers keep the heat in. Mammals and birds can shiver to warm up when they are cold and sweat or pant to cool down when they are hot. But reptiles and amphibians do not have feathers or fur. Their skins are not good insulators, and most have little body fat. They get warmer or cooler depending on the weather outside, and they can only control their body temperature by their behavior.

On a cool morning, a snake crawls from its shelter to seek out a warm rock and bask in the early sun. As the day goes on, the air warms up, and by noon the snake grows uncomfortably hot. To avoid overheating, it moves to a cooler spot, perhaps under

The slow worm is a legless lizard. It looks like a snake, but it's not.

11

WHAT IS THE DIFFERENCE BETWEEN A LEGLESS LIZARD AND A SNAKE?

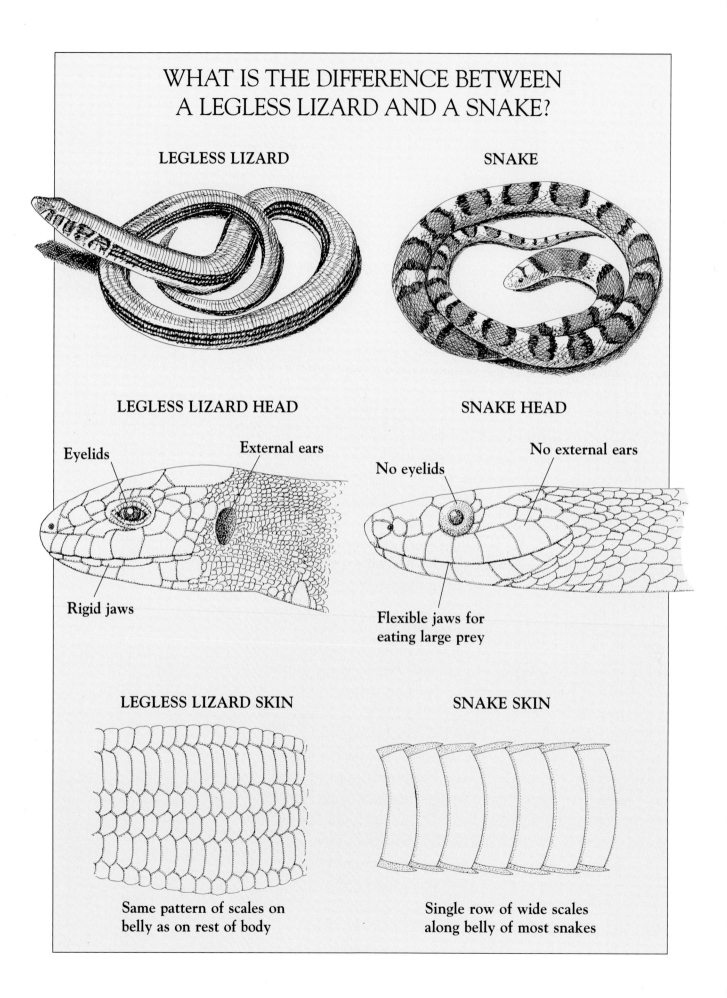

LEGLESS LIZARD

SNAKE

LEGLESS LIZARD HEAD

Eyelids

External ears

Rigid jaws

SNAKE HEAD

No eyelids

No external ears

Flexible jaws for eating large prey

LEGLESS LIZARD SKIN

Same pattern of scales on belly as on rest of body

SNAKE SKIN

Single row of wide scales along belly of most snakes

some shrubs or into a burrow. It stays there until its body grows cool again, signaling the snake to shift its position once more to somewhere warmer. By moving around in this way, a snake can keep its body temperature steady throughout the day. Now you can see why snakes in a zoo don't move much. Their cages are kept at a constant temperature, and they don't need to hunt for food. There's no need for them to do anything more than stay where they are.

The term *cold-blooded* is not an accurate one, because a reptile's blood may not be any colder than yours or mine. A better word is *ectothermic*, meaning "outside heat," because the main source of a reptile's body heat is outside its body. Warm-blooded animals are called *endothermic*, meaning "inside heat," because the main source of their body heat is inside their bodies.

Knowing how a reptile's body works helps us to understand much about its way of life. For example, food is a source of energy for all animals. But because reptiles don't use their food energy to produce body heat, they don't need as much food as birds and mammals do. A snake can get all the energy it needs from only two or three meals a month. For this reason, snakes and lizards can live in harsh environments such as deserts, where there is too little food to allow most mammals and birds to survive.

One disadvantage of relying on the sunshine for their heat is that snakes and other reptiles become slow and sluggish when it gets cold. Although a few snakes live as far north as the Arctic, there are no large snakes there. A large snake would need to spend several hours lying in the northern sun before its body got warm enough to let it start hunting. All the world's largest snakes live in the tropics, where the air temperature is high enough year-round to let them stay active both day and night.

Snake Anatomy

Why are snakes' tongues always flicking in and out? How do some snakes find their prey without seeing it, hearing it, or smelling it? Where does a snake's poison come from? How do snakes move? Answers to questions such as these depend on knowing something about a snake's body and how it is built.

SKELETON AND SKIN

The first thing you notice about a snake is that it is long and thin. It is little more than a head, a stretched-out body, and a tail. If you had X-ray eyes to look inside the snake, you would see a skeleton made up only of a skull and a long backbone with dozens of ribs attached to it. The backbone of a very big snake may have four hundred or more spine bones called *vertebrae* – as compared with the thirty-three that make up a human spine. (You can feel your vertebrae by running your fingers up and down the middle of your back.) Even an average-size snake has more than a hundred of these bones, which are connected to each other by joints. The large number of joints in its backbone lets a snake bend and coil its body in every direction.

Every vertebra between the head and the tail has a pair of long, thin, curved ribs that run around the sides of the snake's body. Each rib is joined to the ones in front and back of it by muscles, forming a tube of bone and muscle that protects the snake's internal organs. Because snakes do not have limbs, they do not need pelvic bones or shoulder bones. As mentioned earlier, however, the skeletons of some snakes have small remains of the pelvic bones and hind leg bones that snakes' ancestors once had. No snakes have shoulder bones or arm bones.

The prairie rattlesnake, like most snakes, has a flexible spine made up of more than a hundred separate bones and joints.

Snakes vary greatly in shape and appearance. Some are as thin as a pencil. Others have thick, powerful bodies as much as three feet around. Burrowing snakes have rounded, tube-shaped bodies, whereas ground-living snakes are slightly flattened. Some species, such as rattlesnakes, have distinct heads and necks. Others, such as blind snakes, have blunt heads that look much like their tails. Pythons and vipers have relatively short tails, whereas the tails of some slender tree snakes are longer than their bodies. Tree snakes wrap their long tails around the branches of trees to help them climb.

How can you tell where a snake's body ends and its tail begins? It's easier to see if the snake is upside-down. On the underside of most snakes is a single row of broad scales, called *scutes*. The scutes cross the snake's belly widthwise and overlap one another from the front of the body to the back (see the drawing on page 18). The scutes end where the tail starts, and the body narrows slightly at this point. The last scute is larger than the others and covers a small opening called the *cloaca*, where the body's wastes pass out.

Scutes help some snakes crawl by gripping the ground like the tread of a Caterpillar tractor. But not all snakes have scutes. Most burrowing snakes and many species that live in water have belly scales that are similar in size and shape to the scales covering the rest of their bodies.

A snake's scales grow out of its skin. You can sometimes see the skin after a snake has eaten a large meal: its swollen body pushes apart the scales, exposing the skin underneath. Scales are made of the same material (called *keratin*) that forms the claws, hoofs, fur, and feathers of other animals, as well as your own nails and hair.

Snake skin feels dry to the touch. The scales may be smooth or rough, depending on the species of

The rough scales of this rat snake help it climb even the smoothest-looking tree trunks.

snake. The differences in scale texture are probably connected with the snake's way of life. For example, coral snakes spend much of their time under logs or in burrows and have smooth, glossy scales that let them slip easily through tight spaces. Rat snakes, which often climb trees, have rough scales with a little ridge, or *keel*, running down the middle of each. The ridges help the snake get a grip on small cracks and crevices in the bark of a tree trunk.

Scales cover every part of a snake's body, including its eyes. Snakes do not have eyelids, but each eye is covered and protected by a clear, bubblelike scale called a *spectacle*. Without eyelids, snakes cannot blink or close their eyes. They look as if they are always staring, even when they are asleep.

Snake skin, like our own, gets dried out, wetted, windblown, and generally roughed up during the animal's day-to-day life. We grow new skin and shed little flakes of our old skin constantly, but snakes shed their entire outer layer of skin at once.

Skin shedding takes place after a new set of scales has grown in underneath. A few days before it peels, the snake's old skin appears dull, dry, and rougher than usual. The snake's eyes become clouded by a white haze as its old spectacles gradually loosen. Snakes get sluggish and withdrawn at this time. They often seek out damp hiding places where they can relieve their itchy skin. They may get bad-tempered and refuse to feed, perhaps because they cannot see well.

The old skin comes away first around the mouth. The snake rubs its jaws and chin against rocks or rough bark and crawls among vegetation to help push off the loosened skin. The paper-thin layer of outer skin rolls back from the head over the body and comes off inside out, just as your sock does if you grip it at the top and peel it down over your foot. It usually takes several hours for the snake to shed its skin completely from head to tail.

You may be lucky enough to find an old snake skin caught on a bush all in one piece, although it often tears into two or three large bits. It is crinkly, thin, and delicate, and if you hold it up to the light, you can see through it. Every detail of the old scales is preserved, including the clear, round spectacles that were over the eyes. Once out of its old skin, the snake appears bright, shiny, and freshly colored.

Young, fast-growing snakes may shed their skin three times a year. A baby snake may get rid of its first skin when it is only two weeks old. Full-grown adults shed no more than once or twice a year.

A shedding grass snake shows its new skin under the old.

HOW DO SNAKES MOVE?

Lateral undulation

Most snakes move in an S-shaped path. Each curve temporarily anchors part of the body to the ground and lets the snake push forward from it. This is called lateral undulation. If you look at snake tracks made in soft soil, you can see small ridges of earth heaped up at the outer edge of each curve. This is where the snake's body has pushed against the ground to get a forward thrust.

Locomotion using belly scutes

Large, heavy snakes use a different type of motion. They commonly crawl slowly forward in a more or less straight line. The forward thrust is produced by the snake's belly scutes. Each scute is attached to two or more pairs of ribs by muscles. The muscles are used to tilt the scutes at different angles and to pull them back and forth. When the snake moves, each scute is first lifted up slightly, then moved forward, pushed down onto the ground, and pulled backward. When the anchored scute is pulled backward, it hitches the snake forward over it. Scutes are coordinated to move together in groups, so wavelike ripples of motion flow along the snake's underside as it crawls along.

Underside

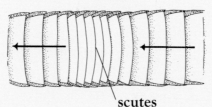

scutes

Side view

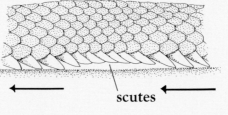

scutes

Sidewinding

One of the oddest-looking ways of getting around is by sidewinding. Snakes use this method to move over areas of shifting sand, where the usual S-shaped motion would simply push the sand away from them and leave them sprawling. A sidewinder moves by throwing its body forward a portion at a time. The front end arches up first and lands ahead. When its neck hits the ground, the snake twists the rest of its body forward, clear of the ground, and places it just beside and in front of its head. Before the tail has landed, the snake throws its head up again, going forward and sideways.

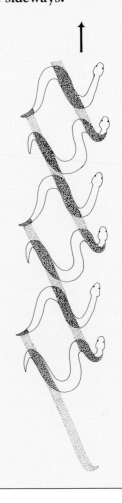

Accordianlike movement

Burrowing snakes and some tree-climbing snakes use an accordianlike action to creep along, folding and then straightening their bodies. To move along a wide burrow, a snake bunches up the front of its body in loops that press against the tunnel's sides. Holding on with these loops, it pulls its tail forward. Then it does the opposite. It folds its tail end into loops that touch the tunnel wall, while it straightens its head end and moves forward.

Tree boas do much the same among branches. They wrap their tails around one branch and stretch their heads forward to another. Then they loop their front ends around the second branch and pull their tails up after them.

Swimming

Snakes swim using the same S-shaped motion used on land. The tails of sea snakes are adapted to a life of swimming by being broad and flattened from side to side. This gives them more pushing power against the water, like the blade of an oar.

Gliding

A few snakes can fly – or at least glide. To get from one tree to another a few feet away, the snake climbs to a high branch and leaps into the air. Once airborne, it spreads its long ribs, pulls in its belly, and stiffens its body to make a wide, concave undersurface. Turned into a sort of parachute, the snake angles down to the branches or trunk of the neighboring tree. On landing, it folds its ribs back and looks like a regular snake.

A northern copperhead shows how flexible its jaws are. Snakes can open their mouths wider than any other animal can.

JAWS AND FANGS

The snake's jaws are a key to its successful way of life. Unlike our own fairly rigid jaws, the jaws of most snakes are amazingly flexible. Snakes not only use their jaws like hands, to grasp and handle food, they can practically disconnect them to eat, letting the snakes swallow animals much larger than their own heads.

A snake's lower jaw is connected to the upper jaw at the back by a pivoting hinge. Using this hinge, the snake can drop its lower jaw down before swinging its mouth open, allowing it an enormous gape of nearly 150° – about three times as great as we can manage when the dentist asks us to open wide.

The lower jaw of a snake is not a single, solid piece of bone as ours is. Instead, the two halves of the jaw are joined together at the front by a stretchable ligament, like an elastic band. Each half of the jaw can be moved back and forth by itself, and the two halves can be separated and spread wide apart.

Most snakes have slender teeth as sharp as needles. The teeth usually curve backward. This helps prevent prey from escaping, for many snakes swallow their victims alive. Poisonous snakes have long, specialized teeth called *fangs* growing from their upper jaws. They use these fangs to puncture the skin of their prey and inject *venom* (poison). The venom itself is produced and stored in glands at the base of the fangs.

There are three main types of fangs, found in three different types of snakes. The simplest are those found in rear-fanged snakes, such as the African boomslang. These snakes have from one to three fangs on each side at the back of their upper jaws. Each fang has a deep groove in its surface, down which venom trickles when the snake bites into its prey. The second type of fangs is found in members of the cobra family (see page 37). These snakes have one pair of fangs at the front of their jaws. Each fang has a hollow tube down its center and works like a miniature hypodermic needle. The third type of fangs is found in members of the viper family, including rattlesnakes (see page 39). Vipers have a pair of hollow fangs at the front of their upper jaws that can be folded back against the roof of the mouth when they are not using them. When a viper attacks, its fangs spring down and out. The snake stabs rather than bites its prey, and muscles around its venom glands squeeze poison through the fangs and into the wound.

A snake's teeth, including its fangs, drop out individually from time to time. New teeth are always growing in just behind the old ones to replace them. Fangs are thin and quite delicate and may need replacing as often as every two weeks when the snake is hunting frequently.

Venomous snakes, such as this eastern diamondback rattlesnake, make new venom constantly in glands behind their fangs.

21

A Mojave rattlesnake uses its tongue to detect smell and taste.

ORGANS AND SENSES

Because of a snake's unusual body shape, its internal organs are arranged a little differently from those in other vertebrates (animals with backbones). Many organs, such as the heart and liver, are long and narrow. Paired organs, such as the kidneys, are not positioned side by side but overlap, one behind the other. Some organs are missing or reduced in size. For example, most snakes have only one lung (the right lung), which runs halfway down the body and does the work of two. In species with both lungs, the left lung is less than half the size of the right.

Snakes depend on their sense organs to find prey and avoid enemies. But their senses are not the same as ours. Sight and hearing are much less important to them than smell and taste.

Snakes are often said to be deaf. They have no outside ears or eardrums and cannot hear airborne sounds as we do. However, there is some evidence that they can use their lungs for hearing. Snakes sense sound waves coming through the air as tiny vibrations on their skin. These vibrations then travel from the skin through the air-filled lung to the nerves of the snake's inner ear. Snakes can also hear low-frequency vibrations that travel through the ground. A snake picks up these vibrations through its underside, which is always in contact with the ground. To find out what it might be like to "hear" this way, plug your ears, rest your chin on a tabletop, and then have someone tap underneath the table. The vibrations will go to your inner ear through your jawbones.

Vibrations from a moving animal can travel a long distance through the ground. A snake can tell from these vibrations if an animal is approaching it or going away. It can tell if the animal is big, and possibly dangerous, or small, and possibly dinner.

Because a sense of vision is not much use underground, most burrowing snakes have tiny eyes. Some have eyes that detect only light and darkness and are otherwise blind. Other snakes have reasonably good eyesight, but what they can see from a few inches off the ground is limited. Coachwhip snakes, which are long and slender, are one of the few snakes that hunt mainly by sight, raising their front ends high above the ground to look around. For most snakes, however, the eyes are probably most important for detecting something moving nearby.

Tree snakes have the best eyesight among snakes. Some species have a groove running along the length of the snout in front of each eye. These grooves let them look forward, unlike other snakes, which can see only to either side of the head. By sighting along its grooves, a tree snake can focus both eyes at once on a bird in front of it. The overlapping images give it a good sense of depth and distance, helping it to hunt among the branches of a tree.

You can tell if a snake is active by day or by night from the shape of its pupils. Snakes that hunt during daylight, such as the common garter snake, usually have round pupils. Night hunters, such as the timber rattlesnake, have narrow, vertical slits in their eyes, like those of a cat. A vertical pupil can be closed more

Tree snakes have good eyesight. Grooves along the snout of this long-nosed whip snake let it focus directly ahead.

23

tightly than a circular one, protecting the light-sensitive back of the eye when a night prowler comes out by day to bask in the sun. Some tree snakes have unusual horizontal pupils. These may help them get a wider field of view when looking to the front. It is difficult to know if snakes see color, although there is evidence that at least some of them can.

When a snake crosses a trail made recently by a mouse, its long, forked tongue starts to flick in and out more rapidly. The snake's tongue is not a sting, as some people think. It is part of the snake's most important sense – a combination of taste and smell. Snakes use their tongues to "taste the air," although they do not have taste buds as people do.

Inside a snake's mouth, the tongue is protected within a tough sheath that runs back under the windpipe. A snake can put out its tongue without opening its mouth, through a small notch in its upper lip. While hunting, snakes flick out their tongues every few seconds. The waving tongue picks up tiny chemical particles of scent from the air or ground. When the tongue is drawn back, its tip is wiped against a taste-sensing organ in the roof of the snake's mouth.

This special tasting organ is named *Jacobson's organ*, after the Danish scientist who first described it in 1809. It contains lots of nerve endings for analyzing tastes and smells, and it opens into the mouth by two small holes, like nostrils. The snake presses one fork of its tongue tightly into each opening – which explains why the tongue is forked.

In addition to the Jacobson's organ, snakes also have nostrils and a regular sense of smell. They probably use their nostrils to detect stronger or more distant scents, and their tongues to track fainter, closer smells. Snakes also use their tongues to find other snakes at mating time and to detect nearby

A special organ located in the holes behind the rattlesnake's nostrils detects heat.

enemies. When next to an object, they use their tongues to touch and feel.

Two holes in the snout of a rattlesnake, between its eyes and nostrils, are clues to a remarkable sense found only in some snakes and in no other animals. The holes are heat-sensitive pits, used to find prey by tracking body heat. These organs are best developed in a group of snakes called pit vipers (which include rattlesnakes, copperheads, and water moccasins), although some boas and pythons have similar heat-detecting areas along their lips.

Each pit is lined with nerve endings that are sensitive to changes in air temperature. Heat sensors are particularly useful for hunting at night or down dark tunnels. Because there is one pit on each side of its head, the snake can use tiny differences in the temperature sensed by each pit to pinpoint exactly where its prey is hiding. By slowly moving its head from side to side and by responding to temperature changes of a fraction of a degree, the snake can strike accurately at its victim without seeing it at all.

Snake Families

The yellow rat snake is a member of the Colubridae, the largest snake family.

Zoologists divide the world's twenty-six hundred or so species of snakes into about ten groups, called families. The snakes in each family all have something in common that makes them different from the snakes in other families. Some families have only a few species; others have hundreds.

What sorts of things make some snakes different from others? One important difference is whether or not they have the remains of a pelvis and hind limbs in their skeletons. Snakes that do have these tiny bones are considered more primitive in this respect than snakes that do not. Another difference is whether or not they live underground. Burrowing snakes are thought to be an older group, since the first snakes evolved from burrowing reptiles. The snakes in some families are all poisonous, and in other families they are all nonpoisonous. The biggest family, however – called the Colubridae – includes both poisonous and nonpoisonous species.

Remember that these families are made up by people, and some species of snakes don't fit neatly into one group or another. Scientists do not always agree about what makes up a particular family, and they discuss these classifications back and forth among themselves. As people discover more about each species of snake, scientists may slightly change the way they classify them.

Each species and family has a Latin name that is used by scientists around the world. These names help avoid the confusion that sometimes happens when common English names are used. For example, a single species may have several different common names, such as the moccasin, which is also called the

The timber rattlesnake lives in forests on North America's east coast. It is a member of the Viperidae family.

THE FAMILIES OF SNAKES

Scientists are always revising their classification systems for animals – and they don't always agree among themselves. This table shows the major families of snakes that are recognized by most scientists at the present time. Many scientists would probably suggest changes to the list. Some would argue that as many as five or six families could be added. The list is certainly not a final one. In fact, there can be no such thing as long as scientists continue their studies.

Notice that all the family names end in the letters *idae*. This is pronounced "ee-dee." For example, *Boidae* is pronounced "BO-ee-dee."

Family name	Common names	Approximate number of species
Typhlopidae	blind snakes, worm snakes	300
Leptotyphlopidae	thread snakes	80
Aniliidae	false coral snake	1
Xenopeltidae	sunbeam snake	1
Uropeltidae	shieldtail snakes	40
Boidae	boas, pythons	70
Colubridae	many different snakes (poisonous and nonpoisonous)	1,800
Elapidae	cobras, mambas, coral snakes	190
Hydrophiidae	sea snakes	50
Viperidae	vipers, rattlesnakes	150

cottonmouth. Also, several different species share some common names, such as blind snake, worm snake, or coral snake.

A cottonmouth swallows a fish. Note the white lining that gives the snake its name.

TYPHLOPIDAE FAMILY

These small, burrowing snakes live in warmer parts of the world, from Africa and Australia to Southeast Asia and Central and South America. They are called blind snakes because their eyes are tiny and of little use. Blind snakes have thick bodies with small heads and short, blunt tails.

    The biggest blind snakes grow to be more than two feet long, but most are about eight inches in length. They feed on insects and other small creatures in the soil. Blind snakes have small, smooth, even-size scales that help them move easily through the ground.

LEPTOTYPHLOPIDAE FAMILY

Thread snakes, or slender blind snakes, live in dry, tropical regions of Africa, Central and South America, Mexico, the southwestern United States, and parts of the Middle East. They are primitive snakes, with a pelvis and the remains of hind limbs. Like blind snakes, they are small, harmless, burrowing insect-eaters that rarely come up to the surface of the ground. Thread snakes are often found feeding in termite or ant nests, where their close-fitting scales protect them from being bitten. Thread snakes have teeth in their lower jaws only, while most blind snakes have teeth in their upper jaws only. The thread snake family includes the smallest snakes in the world, only four inches long when full-grown.

ANILIIDAE FAMILY

This family has only one species, the false coral snake, found in the tropical regions of South America. Like other burrowing snakes, this species has tiny eyes, a cylindrical body, and a short tail that make it look as if it has a head at both ends. It spends most of its time underground, hunting slender prey such as lizards and legless amphibians. The false coral snake is three feet or less in length. Its bright red-and-black bands resemble the markings of a venomous coral snake. It gives birth to live young.

XENOPELTIDAE FAMILY

The sunbeam snake, a burrowing snake about three feet long, is also put in a family of its own. It lives in India and parts of Southeast Asia. It has a compact head that helps it to burrow through soft earth in search of frogs, mice, other snakes, and lizards. The sunbeam snake is rarely seen, as it is dull in color and hunts at night. It gets its name from the bright, shiny reflection that its scales produce under certain lights. Unlike most other snakes, the sunbeam snake has two working lungs, although the left lung is about half the size of the right.

UROPELTIDAE FAMILY

The small family of shieldtail snakes is found only in India and Sri Lanka. From eight to twenty inches long, these snakes appear similar to other burrowing snakes, except that their tails may be cone shaped, or flattened at a rooflike angle, as if they had been sliced off. Some species have spines and crests on their tails.

The anaconda is not quite the longest snake in the world, but it is the bulkiest.

A shieldtail snake may use its tail to anchor its rear end as it straightens its body to push through the ground, or it may use its tail as a defensive shield to plug the entrance to its burrow. Shieldtails feed on earthworms and other small animals. Unlike most burrowing snakes, they do not lay eggs but give birth to live young. Many shieldtails are brightly colored.

BOIDAE FAMILY

This family includes the biggest snakes in the world, as well as several smaller species. Its members are not poisonous but kill by constriction, wrapping their coils around and suffocating their prey. Boas and pythons have more primitive characteristics than other nonburrowing snakes.

Boas and pythons differ in several ways, and some scientists put them in two separate families. The most obvious difference is in where they live. Most boas live in Central and South America; pythons live in Africa, Southeast Asia, and Australia. Also, boas give birth to live young, whereas pythons lay eggs.

The biggest species of boa is the anaconda. These giants, which can grow to more than twenty feet in length and weigh more than three hundred pounds, spend much of their time near the edges of rivers and swamps. They lie in wait in shallow water for water birds and mammals that come to drink.

Like other pythons, the Indian python is not poisonous but kills its prey by constriction.

The most famous species of boa is the boa constrictor, which many people imagine to be large and dangerous. In fact, boa constrictors average less than eight feet long and are no threat to people. They are good swimmers and live in a variety of habitats, from tropical rain forests to dry grasslands to small offshore islands. Their color may be brown, yellow, or orange, with irregular dark blotches.

The emerald tree boa, as its name suggests, is green and lives in trees. Adults have creamy spots and lines that make them hard to see among the branches and leaves. Their young are bright yellow or pink, but they slowly change to the adult color as they grow. These boas rest tightly coiled around branches. They reach about six feet in length and feed on birds, squirrels, and lizards.

Two species of boas live in the United States. The rubber boa ranges through the western states and as far north as southern British Columbia, Canada. It is small (eighteen inches long), heavily built, and dark brown in color. Rubber boas live in damp forests, burrowing under fallen logs and loose bark. The attractive rosy boa lives in the desert and scrubland of Arizona and southern California. Rosy boas are gray to rose colored, striped, and less than three feet long. Like rubber boas, they have short, blunt tails and coil themselves into a tight ball when threatened.

The rubber boa is one of two species of boa that lives in North America.

Several of the twenty-seven species of pythons grow to be more than twenty-five feet long. The reticulated python, found in Southeast Asia, is probably the world's longest snake. A specimen killed in 1912 measured thirty-two feet, nine inches. Although they are very long, pythons do not have the heavy, bulky build that most boas have. They eat mainly small mammals such as rats, but may sometimes catch larger prey such as pigs, deer, and even people.

The ball python, also known as the royal python, lives in dry forests and savannas in West Africa. When frightened, this snake coils into a tight ball, with its head well protected in the middle of its coils. The defensive snake can be rolled along the ground.

The green tree python is much like the emerald tree boa of South America. It lives in New Guinea and spends most of its life in the treetops. Like the tree boa, it has a long, *prehensile* tail – one that can be used to grip tightly around branches. It also has long front teeth, which help it to catch fast-moving prey such as birds. It even rests in the same way as the emerald tree boa, tightly coiled around a branch with its head lying on top in the middle of its loops. These two species are not closely related and live in different parts of the world, but they have evolved to look and behave alike in their similar forest environments.

33

Although the garter snake is the most widely-distributed reptile in North America, some species of garter snake, including the San Francisco variety (above), are endangered.

COLUBRIDAE FAMILY

About three-quarters of all snakes are in the Colubridae family, which includes species in every part of the world where snakes are found. Some colubrids live on the ground, some live in trees, some are water snakes, and some can live in all three habitats. Most members of this family eat a variety of small prey, but a few species have specialized diets. For example, there are snail-eating snakes, crab-eating snakes, and egg-eating snakes.

The majority of colubrid snakes are non-poisonous. They include such familiar species as garter snakes, rat snakes, corn snakes, fox snakes, grass snakes, smooth snakes, water snakes, racers, king snakes, hognose snakes, and gopher snakes. Many of these species are commonly seen around farmland. Their prey includes insects, slugs, mice, rats, and young birds.

If you happen to see a small, slender snake in a vacant lot or a park or beside a road, there is a good chance that it will be a garter snake. There are more than twenty species of garter snakes in North America. They vary in length from less than a foot to a maximum of about four feet. The common garter snake is found from the east coast to the west and as far north as the Yukon and southern Alaska, making it one of the most northerly snakes in the world. Garter snakes live in a wide variety of habitats, but they are especially common near creeks, marshes, and small streams. Most garter snakes have three stripes along their bodies. This pattern gave them their name, since it resembles the striped pattern seen on the old-fashioned elastic garters once used to hold up stockings.

Rat snakes, and the closely related chicken snakes and corn snakes, are common large snakes in

The king snake eats mainly other snakes.

many countries in the world. They may reach eight feet long but average between three and five feet. They have blunt heads and stout bodies that are squarish in cross section. Many of them hunt at night, catching, rats, mice, and other small prey. They are good climbers and can even crawl up smooth-barked trees in search of squirrels, birds, or eggs. Rat snakes vary in color in different parts of the world. Adults may be mainly black, yellow, green, or pink.

Racers and whip snakes are similar in length to rat snakes, but their bodies are slender and round rather than stout and squarish like the bodies of rat snakes. They are found in the United States, Europe, and Asia. Racers have a reputation for moving extremely fast. Their slim build, quick reactions, and darting movements make them appear extra speedy, but in measured tests they don't move much faster than other snakes – about three-and-a-half miles per hour.

King snakes get their name as head of the snake world because their food consists mainly of snakes – including other king snakes. They kill their prey by constriction and are immune to the toxins of venomous

The long, thin vine snake can swallow its prey while hanging head-down from a branch.

species. In addition to eating snakes, they feed on lizards, mice, and birds. King snakes are found in the southern United States, Mexico, and Central America. They are three to four feet long when adult, and many species are brightly colored with banded patterns.

A close relative of the king snake is the milk snake, which lives in the central and eastern United States and southeastern Canada. Milk snakes are most active at night. The name of these snakes comes from an old farmers' tale that they suck milk from cows, but there is no evidence to show that this story is true.

Poisonous colubrids are all rear-fanged snakes (see page 21). Few of them have powerful venom, however, and they must get a good grip on their prey to work their poison into it. The poison works mainly to paralyze the prey before it is swallowed. Most rear-fanged colubrids live in trees in tropical regions. They include vine snakes and flying snakes.

Mexican vine snakes look as though they couldn't swallow anything bigger around than spaghetti. They grow as long as five feet but are no thicker than a pen. They are very muscular, however, and can hang for hours from a branch, looking like a twig or a creeper. Their well-camouflaged appearance makes them difficult to see, both for predators and for their prey, which consists mostly of lizards.

The boomslang of Africa is thought to be the most dangerous rear-fanged snake. It can open its mouth wider than most other colubrid snakes, so it can grip prey with its rear fangs and inject venom more easily when it bites. Its venom is also very strong. Boomslangs grow as long as five feet and are mainly green, brown, black, yellow, or gray. They spend most of their time in trees, waiting motionless for a passing lizard or chameleon. A boomslang is sometimes so still and well camouflaged that a bird may perch on it.

ELAPIDAE FAMILY

The Australian king brown snake is venomous and extremely aggressive.

Elapids are poisonous snakes that live in the tropics around the world. The family includes cobras in Asia and Africa, mambas in Africa, coral snakes in the Americas, and all the venomous snakes in Australia. Australian elapids include the tiger snake, king brown snake and taipan. All elapids have hollow, poisonous fangs at the front of their upper jaws.

The king cobra is the world's largest poisonous snake, growing to a record length of just over eighteen feet. It lives in India, southern China, and Southeast Asia. Like other cobras, when it is startled or angry the king cobra rears up and spreads out the long, movable ribs in its neck to form a "hood." When it is not displaying in this way to scare off predators, the ribs and skin of its neck lie flat against its body and it looks like a regular snake. King cobras are shy – and rare. They eat mostly snakes.

The Indian cobra is widespread in Asia. It is the species commonly kept by snake charmers. Indian cobras grow to between four and five feet long and have particularly wide hoods. Their hoods are made

The beautiful coral snake has one of the most toxic venoms of all American snakes, but it is rarely seen. It is a relative of the cobras.

even more dramatic by one or two large "eyespot" markings on the back. The dark circles, rimmed by a paler color, give the snake its other name – the spectacled cobra.

Several cobras in Africa do more than show a scary hood to frighten away enemies. They spray venom at their attackers' eyes. These snakes are called spitting cobras. When threatened, they raise their front ends and force venom out of small slits at the tips of their fangs. Spitting cobras aim for the eyes and are accurate to distances up to six feet. The venom is dangerous only if it enters a cut or gets in the eyes, where it causes a burning pain and blindness that may last for several hours. Spitting cobras spit venom only to defend themselves, not to catch prey.

Mambas are often feared because of their great speed and powerful venom, which can kill a person in ten minutes. There are four species of these African snakes – the common mamba, the black mamba, and two green mambas. All are slim and grow from ten to fourteen feet long. Green mambas live in trees; common mambas and black mambas live mostly on the ground.

The only elapid snakes in North America are the coral snakes. There are about fifty species, all of which grow two to four feet long. They are not commonly seen, as they often burrow and hunt at night. They have fast-acting venom but rarely bite people. Many coral snakes have distinctive patterns of rings in black, red, and white or yellow colors that look as though they were freshly put on with enamel paints. Their brilliant colors and pattern protect them because they are easily recognized by predators, which stay away rather than risk being bitten. Several harmless species in other families, such as the false coral snake, look similar and are often mistaken for poisonous snakes.

HYDROPHIIDAE FAMILY

One of the most unusual families of snakes is the Hydrophiidae. Their Latin name means "water loving." This group includes snakes that are born in the sea and spend their entire lives there, as well as snakes that spend part of their time on land. Most sea snakes live in the South Pacific and Indian oceans. Despite stories of giant sea serpents, sea snakes are not especially large. Most are four to five feet long, and the biggest grow to little more than nine feet. They are poisonous snakes with hollow front fangs, and many scientists group them with the Elapidae family.

Little is known about the lives of sea snakes. They are most often seen when caught in fishing nets, though they have also been encountered in large numbers basking near the surface of the sea. They feed on fish and can stay submerged for several hours before coming up to breathe. Their flattened tails make them powerful swimmers. The yellow-bellied sea snake is often found far from land in the Pacific Ocean. This species cannot move easily on land and gives birth to its live young in the calmer waters of sheltered bays. The common sea snake, however, comes on land to lay eggs.

VIPERIDAE FAMILY

Vipers take top prize for efficient poisoning equipment. Their long, hollow fangs are hinged to their upper jaws so they can be folded back when not in use and flipped forward when the snake strikes (see page 21). There are two main divisions of this family. Typical vipers and adders live in Europe, Asia, and Africa. Pit vipers (which include rattlesnakes, moccasins, and copperheads) live mainly in North and South America.

The gaboon viper lives in the rain forests of central Africa and has the longest fangs of any snake. A six-foot-long gaboon viper may have two-inch-long fangs – almost the length of its head. Another African viper, the puff adder, is responsible for many of the

The gaboon viper is found in the forests of central Africa. Its fangs are longer than any other snake's.

snakebites in Africa. It gets its name from the display it uses to protect itself. When threatened, the puff adder inflates its lungs and swells up like a long balloon. Then it hisses with a loud puffing sound that can be heard some distance away.

Pit vipers differ from other vipers by having heat-sensitive pits on their snouts, which they use to locate their prey (see page 25). Included in the pit viper group are more than twenty-five species of rattlesnakes, the most common poisonous snakes in the United States. Rattlesnakes are among the easiest snakes to identify, with the dry, bare scales at the ends of their tails, which they rattle as a warning. Rattlesnakes range in size from the two-foot-long pygmy rattlesnake to the eight-foot-long eastern diamondback. The diamondback is the largest venomous snake in North America.

Most rattlesnakes live in the dry, hot states of the South and the West, but the timber rattlesnake is common in damp forests and valleys along the east coast. The sidewinder is a species of rattlesnake that is adapted to move over loose sand (see page 18). It is also known as the horned rattlesnake because it has a small, projecting "horn" sticking out over each eye. These projections probably help to protect the eyes when the snake is buried in the sand.

The cottonmouth, or water moccasin, is a pit viper that lives in swamps and other wet areas in the southern United States. It grows more than three feet long and eats mainly frogs, fish, and small turtles. The cottonmouth is usually sluggish and reluctant to move when disturbed. It gives a warning display to intruders by opening its jaws and showing the white inside of its mouth that gives it its name.

The fer-de-lance is probably the most dangerous snake in South America. It is a large pit viper that

The sidewinder is sometimes called a horned rattlesnake because of the projections above its eyes.

grows up to eight feet long. Its natural home is the forest floor, but it may also be found around plantations, where it feeds on rats.

The largest viper – and the longest venomous snake in the Americas – is the bushmaster. Unusually big bushmasters may grow up to twelve feet long, but they are not as heavily built as most pit vipers. Bushmasters live in the forests of Central and South America but are rarely seen, as they hunt mostly at night. They are the only American pit vipers that lay eggs, rather than giving birth to live young.

The Hunt for Food

A snake lies coiled on the forest floor, nearly hidden among the fallen leaves. Its eyes stare, unblinking. Its flicking tongue detects the faint odor of rats, which run at night along a narrow trail that passes only inches from the snake. It has been waiting in this spot for two days and narrowly missed catching a rat the night before.

Now the snake feels small vibrations through its belly as something moves toward it through the woods. The vibrations signal something bigger than a rat, and the snake flicks out its tongue more often to pick up the scent. A shape comes into view on its left, but the snake does not move. The shape grows larger, and the smell of a rabbit grows stronger. The snake can see the animal more clearly now, using its good night vision in the dim light. When the unsuspecting rabbit hops to within striking distance, the snake tenses its muscles for attack, then lunges and bites. After two days of waiting, it's all over in seconds.

All snakes are hunters, catching and eating other animals. But different snakes eat different things and hunt in different ways, depending on the snake's size and species and also on where it lives. Small, burrowing snakes eat earthworms, slugs, termites, and other small animals they find underground. Most sea snakes eat fish. Tree snakes feed on birds, lizards, squirrels, and nestlings. The prey of typical ground-living snakes ranges from frogs, mice, rats, and rabbits all the way up to small antelopes and pigs. Large snakes have even been known to swallow such unlikely prey as leopards and crocodiles. Because the size of the food depends on the size of the snake, young snakes often eat different prey than their parents do. For example, baby

The Malaysian bronzeback strikes quickly – before its prey can strike back or escape.

43

The common egg-eater of eastern Africa swallows a whole egg, breaks it open, squeezes out the contents, and then spits out the shell.

rattlesnakes may eat mostly mice and small lizards. When grown, they can tackle larger animals, such as rabbits and gophers.

Some species of snakes eat a wide variety of food; others specialize in catching a particular type of prey. For example, a group of small snakes commonly called thirst snakes are experts at eating slugs and snails. They have specially adapted jaws that let them pull the body of a snail from its shell. Their upper jaws are short, with four or five sharp teeth. Their lower jaws are long – up to three times as long as the upper jaws – and stick out in front of their snouts. When it finds a snail, a thirst snake grips the shell firmly with the teeth in its upper jaw. Then it pokes its flexible lower jaw deep into the shell, grabs the body of the snail, and scoops it out with a slow, twisting motion.

Several species of African egg-eating snakes also use an amazing adaptation to deal with their favorite food. Before eating, the snake checks the egg with its tongue to make sure it is fresh. Then it coils its body behind the egg to keep it in place and swallows the egg whole. Now comes the interesting part. The snake uses its backbone to crack the eggshell. The vertebrae in its neck have sharp points that face downward into the snake's throat. These points help hold the egg still after it has been swallowed. The snake then arches its neck and presses down sharply on the egg with other, knoblike projections on its neck bones. The knobs crack the shell, and the contents of the egg are squeezed into the snake's stomach. The broken shell itself is not swallowed any further; the snake regurgitates the pieces through its mouth.

Some snakes specialize in eating other snakes. Their victims may include poisonous species and snakes that are longer than themselves. To avoid the risk of turning from predator into prey, most snakes that eat poisonous species are immune to snake venom. Snake-eaters include the king cobra of Asia and the common king snake of North and South America.

Like the snake described at the beginning of this chapter, many snakes wait for their prey to come to them. They lie quietly in ambush for hours or even days beside a rock or in a tree until their dinner approaches. Most of these "armchair hunters" are heavy-bodied and well camouflaged.

Some snakes use a lure to set a trap for their prey. One example is a dull-colored black-and-brown snake that has a thin, lighter-colored tip at the end of its tail. When the snake spots a lizard nearby, it gently wiggles this tip. The movement attracts the attention of the lizard, which comes to investigate the "worm." By the time the lizard realizes its mistake, it is usually too late – it has walked almost into the jaws of the waiting snake. African vine snakes are reported to use a similar trick. Their bodies are camouflaged among the treetops, but they have bright red or yellow tongues with black tips. The flicking tongue attracts birds to what they may think is a tasty insect.

An unusual trap is set by the wart snake, which feeds on fish in lakes and streams in Southeast Asia. These snakes have wartlike bumps covering their skin. The snake uses these rough, hard bumps to help catch its prey. To hunt, the snake lies loosely coiled on the stream bottom, looking like an old rock with interesting cracks and crevices. When a fish swims in to investigate the cracks, the snake tightens its coils, holding the slippery fish in its rough, warty grasp.

Not all snakes kill their prey before eating it. Many small and harmless snakes, which feed on animals such as slugs, worms, and frogs, simply grab

The blunt-nosed viper is well hidden by its color and markings as it lies in wait for its prey.

their prey and swallow it alive. The victim slowly dies from suffocation inside the snake, or from the chemical action of the snake's digestive juices. Because snakes do not chew their prey, victims have been known to survive being swallowed. If a snake is suddenly frightened soon after its meal, it may throw up what it has just swallowed so the snake can escape more quickly. When this happens, the bedraggled but lucky creature that was swallowed may crawl off to live another day.

Most snakes kill their prey before eating it, however, and they usually kill it as quickly as possible. It is important for them to be able to do this, because a victim may counterattack. The snake can easily be trampled, kicked, or bitten by its struggling prey. To avoid possible injury, snakes are experts at speedy attacks that soon put their prey out of action. Snakes have two main methods of killing: constriction and poison.

Constrictors squeeze their prey to death. After seizing an animal in its jaws, a constrictor immediately throws one or more coils around the victim's body. Trapped in an ever-tightening grip, the prey cannot breathe and soon dies of suffocation or shock. Small animals such as rats and mice may die in seconds. Larger animals take a little longer. Once the victim is dead, the snake loosens its stranglehold and begins to eat its meal.

Snakes that use poison to kill are a minority in the snake world. Less than a quarter of all snakes are venomous, and only about one in ten can kill its prey solely by injecting venom. Rear-fanged snakes must get a good grip on their prey and hold onto it firmly for fifteen minutes or more, biting down repeatedly to work their venom into the wound until it takes effect.

The most advanced venomous snakes are the vipers, with their long, hinged fangs. After attacking,

A gaboon viper blends almost perfectly into the leaves and litter on the African forest floor.

a viper quickly recoils and waits in safety for the poison to immobilize its prey. The entire action – strike, bite, and recoil – may take place in less than a second. Death may come in seconds or minutes, depending on the size of the victim and where on the body it was bitten. If the prey crawls away to die, the viper simply follows the victim's scent trail.

Venomous snakes use only a small fraction of the poison stored in their venom glands when they bite their prey. They can bite many times in succession before they run out of venom – and the second and third bites are just as dangerous as the first. Their venom glands continually make more venom to replace what is used.

Snake venom contains many different chemicals and usually has several effects on the victim's body.

The main effect depends on the type of snake. For example, cobra venom acts mostly on an animal's nervous system. It paralyzes the muscles and eventually stops the heart and lungs from working. Venom from vipers affects the blood, breaking down blood cells so they cannot carry oxygen to the tissues. Most venoms contain chemicals that destroy body tissues and help the poison spread faster from one part of the body to another.

A brown snake eats a mouse headfirst so that its legs fold back against its body and it is more easily swallowed.

Snake venom evolved from saliva, and a snake's venom glands are really modified salivary glands. Even the saliva of some nonvenomous snakes is mildly poisonous to their prey. Like our own saliva, venom contains enzymes that start the process of digestion. Venom starts digesting and softening the prey's tissues even before the snake swallows its meal.

Relative to their size, snakes eat bigger meals than any other predator on land. Other meat-eaters, such as wolves and tigers, also kill large prey, but they use claws and teeth to tear it into bite-size chunks before eating. Snakes, however, have no claws, and their needlelike teeth cannot cut, rip, or chew. They use their teeth only to grip, and they must always swallow their prey whole.

With its mouth and throat completely full of food, a snake might have a problem breathing. To overcome this problem, snakes can push their windpipes forward to the very front of their mouths while eating, so the prey does not block air from getting to and from their lungs. Another adaptation that lets snakes swallow huge meals is that they do not have a breastbone – the bone that ribs are joined to at the front of the chest in many animals. Because the snake's ribs are not connected together at the front, they can spread apart and allow the snake's body to widen.

HOW DO SNAKES SWALLOW THEIR PREY?

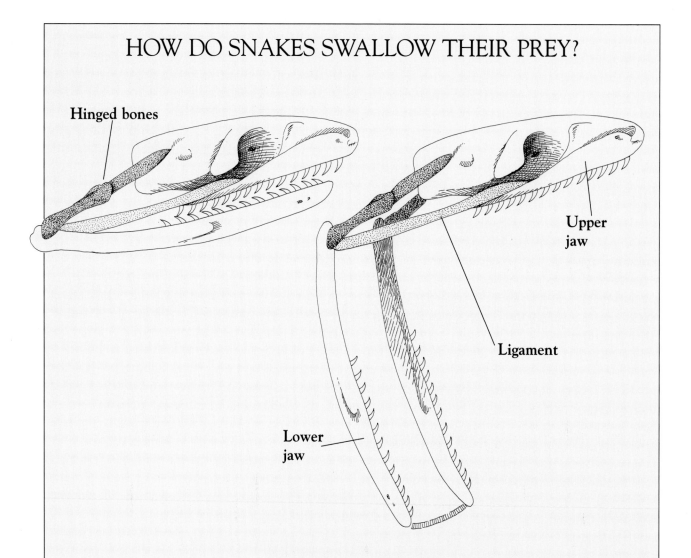

Hinged bones

Upper jaw

Ligament

Lower jaw

Hinged bones, and a stretch-able ligament joining the upper and lower jaws, permit most snakes to open their mouths wider than any other animal.

The two sides of a snake's jaws can move independently of each other. To swallow a meal, the snake slides half of its lower jaw forward, grips the animal, and pulls back; then it does the same with the other half of the jaw. The action is rather like the hand-over-hand motion you might use to haul in a rope. Half of the jaw is always holding on, while the other half is loosened and moving forward to get a new hold. Bit by bit, the snake's jaws "walk" their way over the prey, which slowly disappears from sight.

All of these adaptations of the snake's body let the snake do an impossible-looking trick – swallow a meal wider than itself. One of the biggest meals on record is that of a sixteen-foot African python, which was found with a hundred-and-thirty-pound gazelle inside it.

Typically, a snake can swallow its prey in ten to twenty minutes, although an extra-large meal may take an hour or more to get down. The meal is helped on its way with lots of saliva, produced by salivary glands along the edge of the snake's jaws.

After eating, a snake "yawns" widely to readjust its jaws. Then it looks for a quiet place to rest and digest its meal. The snake's powerful digestive juices can dissolve even small bones and teeth. It may take several days or even weeks to completely digest a single meal, depending on the meal's size and on the temperature (digestion proceeds faster when the snake's body is warm, slower when it is cold). Undigested bits, such as hair, feathers, and fragments of bone, eventually pass out of the snake's cloaca with other waste matter. Snakes do not have bladders and do not produce urine. Instead, their kidneys secrete a strong uric acid that passes out of the body with their dung. The snake's waste is usually fluid and forms a whitish paste on contact with the air.

After eating a meal that may be more than half its own weight, a snake does not have to eat again for a long time. Large snakes in zoos have survived for a year or more on water alone, and a big snake in the wild may get by on five or six good meals a year. The more active a snake is, the more food it needs. A typical, medium-size snake probably eats once every ten to fourteen days on average.

Snake Reproduction

Two male panamint rattlesnakes twist around each other in a test of strength.

Snakes do not have a family life. Males and females do not live together, and parents do not look after their young. At certain times of year, however – usually in the spring – the males and females seek each other out to mate.

Male and female snakes look much alike to our eyes, although females are usually longer. A full-grown female python, for example, may be nearly six feet longer than the biggest male of its species. Male pythons can be identified by the long spurs near the base of their tails (see page 11). In a few species, males and females may have different-colored eyes.

Most snakes are mature and ready to mate when they are between two and five years old. During the breeding season, male snakes find females by following their scent. Females probably produce a special chemical from their skin at breeding time, so the snakes can find each other over long distances using their well developed sense of smell. Often, several males track the same female, and they may meet one another along the route. In some species, when two males meet, they compete with each other in a test of strength. Male rattlesnakes, for example, rear up and face each other, then twist their necks together in a wrestling match. With their bodies pressed close, they sway from side to side, trying to push each other off balance. This sparring and jostling may last half an hour or more. The combat ends when one snake finally gives up and crawls away, leaving the other to pursue the female.

A female snake may mate with several different males. In some species, a female can store sperm from the male inside her body. She can release this sperm to fertilize her eggs several months or even a year after mating, when conditions are most favorable for her

developing young to survive. She may also produce a second or third clutch of eggs without mating again. Some female snakes in captivity have had young after several years of being kept alone.

Some snakes lay eggs and some give birth to live young. Egg-laying snakes include black racers, milk snakes, hognose snakes, pythons, and cobras. These snakes lay their eggs a few weeks after mating, choosing a sheltered spot, such as a mound of sand, a burrow, or a pile of rotting leaves, where the eggs are likely to stay warm and moist. Heaps of compost or manure are favorite sites; gardeners sometimes find a clutch of snake eggs in their compost in the spring. Once the eggs are laid, the female snakes of most species go off and leave them to incubate and hatch by themselves. In some species, however, mother snakes stay with their eggs to protect them against predators and drying winds.

King cobras are the only snakes known to build

The green tree python stays with the eggs it laid until the young have hatched.

53

Two everglades rat snakes hatch from their eggs.

nests. The female cobra piles up a collection of dead leaves, using a loop of her body to drag the material into a mound. She makes two chambers in the nest, one above the other. She lays her eggs in the lower chamber and coils herself in the upper chamber to guard them. In zoos, male cobras have also been seen guarding the eggs.

The number of eggs in a clutch varies from species to species. Small, burrowing snakes may lay only three or four eggs at a time, whereas a giant python may lay as many as a hundred – each as big as a chicken's egg. Most snakes lay between six and thirty eggs. Older females generally have larger clutches than younger ones.

Snake eggs are usually long and narrow, and they vary in color from yellowish or brown to white. Their shells are not brittle like the shells of birds' eggs but rather tough and leathery. In fact, the shells are so flexible that the eggs can be dented or flattened if they press against other eggs or objects around them. Some snakes lay clusters of eggs that stick together, but most lay separate eggs.

The growing embryo inside each egg is nourished by the yolk. The time it takes for the embryo to develop depends on the temperature. Growth is quicker when it is warm and slower when it is cold. On average, though, it takes six to twelve weeks before the eggs hatch. The baby snake cuts its way out of the shell using a tiny, pointed tooth, called an *egg tooth*, which grows from the tip of its upper jaw. A few hours after hatching, the egg tooth drops off.

In snakes that bear live young – such as garter snakes, rattlesnakes, and rosy boas – the fertilized eggs develop inside the mother's body. One advantage of this is that the eggs are better protected than ones that lie on the ground for weeks. A disadvantage is that the mother snake grows heavier as the young snakes develop inside her, making it more difficult for her to hunt or escape predators. She may stay in hiding for much of this period.

Eggs that develop inside the mother snake do not have shells. Each embryo lies inside a clear, thin, tough membrane, much like the one immediately inside the shell of a hen's egg. Just as in eggs that are laid, the embryo gets its nourishment from the yolk of the egg. In a few species, the embryos may exchange some nutrients and wastes with the body of the mother, as the embryos of mammals do.

About twelve weeks after the full-grown snakes mate, baby snakes are ready to enter the world. The number born varies with each species, with anywhere from six to fifty babies in a single litter. The mother snake deposits her babies still inside their transparent sacs, like plastic-wrapped packages. Like the babies that hatch from eggs, each little snake has an egg tooth to help it cut a slit in the membrane and escape.

All baby snakes are able to look after themselves as soon as they are born or hatched. No thicker than a pencil, they feed on earthworms, flies, grasshoppers, ants, and other insects. The babies of venomous snakes have fangs and poison from the moment of birth. They may be small, but their venom typically is more deadly than that of their parents.

The first year of life is dangerous for small snakes. Many of them are eaten by birds, raccoons, opposums, toads, and rats – some or all of which the same snake might eat in turn if it survives and grows bigger. To help them survive, many small snakes have a different color or pattern from their parents'. Their colors camouflage them so they are less likely to be seen by their enemies.

Young snakes that avoid the hazards of life grow fast. In tropical climates, they may double or even triple their length in one year. In cold climates, babies need to grow quickly during the summer so they can survive the winter in hibernation, when growth temporarily stops. Some snakes are mature and nearly full-grown after three years, although slow growth may continue throughout their lives. Others grow more slowly. It is difficult to know how long snakes live in the wild, but some larger snakes kept in zoos have lived as long as thirty years.

Snakes in Their Environment

By the edge of a stream beside a country road, a garter snake slowly stalks a frog, while a small hawk perched on a nearby fence post stares down at the moving snake. The hawk has just flown from a barn along the road, where it watched a large milk snake nosing its way through a hole in the barn door to hunt the rats that eat the grain stored inside. It is nearly sunset. The garter snake and the hawk will soon find shelter for the night, while the milk snake is only just beginning to prowl for food.

Snakes, like all animals, are part of a network of relationships that make up a community of living things, or ecosystem. Every animal and plant in an ecosystem has a place where it lives and a role that it plays. Each animal competes with some and helps others. Snakes, like other animals, eat and in turn are eaten. If any type of snake should suddenly disappear, it would eventually affect all the other animals – and plants – in its ecosystem.

We usually think of a snake's main role as that of a hunter. But most snakes, and especially their eggs and babies, are also food for a wide range of animals. Snakes' enemies include hawks, crows, buzzards, storks, skunks, raccoons, mongooses, rats, wild pigs, baboons, hedgehogs, snapping turtles, crocodiles, and other snakes.

To defend themselves, snakes use a variety of bluffs, warnings, and deceits. One of the most dramatic defenses is used by the hognose snake of North America. At first sight, this harmless snake looks dangerous. If you come across one suddenly, it will puff itself up, hiss loudly, and strike repeatedly toward you. Adding to its fearsome look, the snake flattens its neck to make a cobralike hood. If that

The harmless hognose snake pretends to be dead if attacked.

The king cobra is the giant of venomous snakes. A large individual can rear up almost to the eye level of an adult human when threatened.

doesn't scare you away, the snake will suddenly collapse, roll onto its back with its mouth open, and lie perfectly still. Its imitation of death is a good one; you can even pick the snake up and it will stay quite limp. Because most snake predators appear to prefer healthy, living prey, they usually leave the playacting hognose snake alone. Unfortunately, the bluff breaks down if you turn the snake onto its stomach. The snake will quickly turn itself over again and then lie still once more, as if convinced that it must be belly up to be dead. The hognose snake comes back to life only when all danger has passed.

The most basic defense of many snakes is to avoid being seen in the first place. Many are colored to look like their environment and are difficult to spot when they are not moving. Others stay underground or are active only at night. If they sense danger approaching, they often try to escape into a burrow, crevice, or bush where they cannot be followed.

If an enemy finds it, the snake's next common defense is to attack, or at least pretend to attack. Many snakes, even harmless ones, rear up, strike, and thrash around to confuse or frighten a predator. Some display large eyespots on their scales or open their mouths wide to show patches of bright, startling color.

Snakes use sounds as well as displays as a defense. The bull snake is named for the loud, bellowing noise it makes by forcefully blowing air from its lungs through a thin, vibrating flap at the front of its windpipe. Most snakes can hiss, and some can make popping noises by forcing air through their cloacas. Another unusual noise maker is the rough-scaled viper. It wraps its body in circles and moves one coil quickly against another, making a rasping sound with its scales.

Pine snakes and others that live in forests vibrate their tails among dry leaves to make a rattling sound.

The chief user of this sound, however, is the rattlesnake, which has developed a permanent rattle at the end of its tail to warn away animals that might threaten it. A large rattle may be heard twenty feet away. The rattle is made of dry, hollow scales loosely connected in segments or rings. A new ring is added each time the snake sheds its skin, so older snakes tend to have more rings than younger ones have. But segments also break off, so you cannot accurately tell the age of a rattlesnake from the number of rings on its rattle.

If displays and sounds fail to fend off enemies, snakes try smell. The fox snake gets its name from the musky odor it produces when picked up. Garter snakes put out a strong, vile-smelling liquid from glands near the cloaca. The cottonmouth can spray its musky secretions up to three feet by swishing its tail from side to side. Like skunk scent, snake odors can linger for hours. Some otherwise harmless snakes have secretions that irritate the skin and deter a predator from holding the snake in its mouth.

Like many lizards, a few snakes are able to shed their tails when they are attacked. The broken-off tail wriggles about to distract the predator, while the snake makes its escape. The tail breaks off at a special weak area in the vertebrae. To snap off its tail, the snake violently contracts the muscles on first one side and then the other. The remaining stump eventually develops new skin over it, and a new tail grows back, though it is never as long or as flexible as the original one.

The ultimate defense of poisonous snakes is the threat of their deadly venom. But because the snake takes a risk when it attacks an enemy, it usually prefers to avoid combat if possible. Some snakes do this by using the opposite of camouflage – they advertise themselves with bright colors and markings. The black, yellow, white, and red bands of coral snakes are a good example of such warning patterns. Any predator that has tangled with a coral snake and survived will remember the colors and avoid these snakes in the future.

In colder parts of the world, snakes must defend themselves against the weather as well as against other living things. As fall approaches, snakes move more slowly and are active only when it is warm during the day. It gets harder for them to catch prey and avoid predators. Their body temperature falls, and they look for a safe place where they can spend the winter in hibernation. They must find somewhere deep underground, where there is no risk of frost or subfreezing temperatures that might kill them. In many places, hundreds of snakes of different species hibernate together in caves that are used year after year. They begin to travel to these hibernating dens in late fall.

During hibernation, snakes coil up tightly together for extra protection. Their body processes slow way down, and they remain motionless, as if dead. They stay in this state until the earth begins to warm again in the spring. Their bodies sense the change in climate, and they slowly begin to come to life. On the first warm day after winter, dozens of snakes may appear from cracks in the ground to revive themselves in the weak sunlight. Gradually, they disperse from their winter dens and spread out over the countryside to begin their summer lives once again.

Desert-living snakes not only risk freezing, but they are also at risk from long periods of extremely hot, dry weather. In some areas, they spend the driest months in estivation, a quiet state similar to hibernation. They bury themselves deep down where the sand is cooler and stay there until the worst of the heat is over.

Each spring, thousands of garter snakes leave their hibernating dens and disperse into the surrounding countryside.

The biggest threat of all to every type of snake does not come from other animals or the climate. It comes from people. Snakes are killed by people who are afraid of them. They are killed by vehicles when they come out to lie on a warm road surface. They are killed in some places to be eaten, or to have parts of their bodies used as medicine in folk remedies. Snakes are killed by farmers who want to protect their animals and workers, although many snakes help farmers by eating pests. And they are killed for their skins, which are used to make shoes, belts, and bags.

Humans slaughter hundreds of thousands of snakes each year around the world. But even larger numbers of snakes are threatened by human activities that destroy their homes. As forests are cut, swamps are drained, and countrysides are paved over by roads and buildings, fewer and fewer places remain where snakes and other animals can live undisturbed. Snakes also die when rivers and fields are polluted and when off-road vehicles carve up once-peaceful deserts.

There are still many things that we do not know about the lives of most snakes. Many snakes are rarer today than they once were, and some species are in danger of extinction. People have caused this danger – and people can also change things for the better. If we come to understand snakes and their place in the world, perhaps we will feel the need to save them, rather than harm them.

INDEX

Numbers in italics refer to photographs.

Adders, 39, 40–41
African boomslang, 21, 36
African python, 6, 51
African vine snake, 45–46
Amphibians, 9–10, 11, 13, 30
Anaconda, *31*, 31–32
Anatomy, 14–25
Aniliidae family, 28, 30
Australian king brown snake, *37*, 37

Baby snakes, 55–56, 57
Backbone, 14
Ball (royal) python, 33
Birth, 10, 30, 31, 39, 42, 55–56
Black-and-brown snake, 45
Black mamba, 38
Black racer, 53
Black snake, 37
Blind snake, 15, 28, 29
Blunt-nosed viper, *46*
Boa, 11, 25, 28, 31–33
  constrictor, 32
  emerald tree, 32, 33
  rosy, 33, 55
  rubber, *33*, 33
  tree, 19
Boidae family, 28, 31–33
Bones, 11, 14, 26, 45, 50, 51.
  See also Fossils; Jaws; Skeleton
Boomslang, African, 21, 36
Bronzeback, Malaysian, *43*
Brown snake, Australian king, *37*, 37
Bull snake, 58
Burrowing snakes, 15, 19, 23, 26, 29,
  30–31, 33, 38, 44, 54
Bushmaster, 42

Camouflage, 36, 45, 46, 56, 58, 59.
  See also Color; Markings
Chicken snake, 34–35
Climate, 56. *See also* Habitats;
  Hibernation; Temperature
Climbing, 16, 19, 35
Cloaca, 15, 51, 58
Coachwhip snake, 23
Cobra, 21, 28, 37, 49, 53
  Indian (spectacled), 37–38
  king, 37, 45, 53–54, 58
  spitting, 38
Cold-blooded reptiles, 9, 11, 13
Color, 24, 30, 31, 32, 33, 35, 36, 38, 45,
  46, 54, 56, 58, 59–60. *See also*
  Camouflage; Markings
Colubridae family, 26, 28, 34–36
Common egg-eater, *44*
Common garter snake, 23, 34

Common mamba, 38
Common sea snake, 39
Constriction, 31, 32, 35, 47
Copperhead, 25, 40
  northern, *20*
Coral snake, 16, 28, 29, 30, 37, *38*, 38, 60
  false, 28, 30, 38
Corn snake, 34–35
Cottonmouth (water moccasin), 25, *29*,
  29, 41, 59

Diamondback rattlesnake, eastern, *21*, 41
Diet. *See* Eating; Food; Hunting
Digestion, 49, 51
Displays, 57, 58

Ears, *12*, 22, 23. *See also* Hearing
Eastern diamondback rattlesnake, *21*, 41
Eating, 13, 17, 20, 21, 51. *See also* Food;
  Hunting; Jaws
Ecosystem, snakes and, 57–62
Ectothermic animals, 13
Egg-eater, common, *44*
Egg-eating snakes, 34, 35, *44*, 44–45
Egg-laying snakes, 53–55
Eggs, 9, *10*, 10, 31, 39, 42, 52–55, 57
Egg tooth, 55–56
Elapidae family, 28, 37–38, 39
Embryos, 55
Emerald tree boa, 32, 33
Endothermic animals, 13
Enemies. *See* Predators
Estivation, 60
Everglades rat snake, *54*
Evolution of snakes, 10–11
Eyes/eyesight, *12*, 16–17, 23–24, 29, 30,
  41, 43, 52
Eyespots, 58

False coral snake, 28, 30, 38
Families of snakes, 26–42
Fangs, 21, 37, 38, 39, 40, 47–48
Fat, body, 11
Female snakes, 52–53, 54
Fer-de-lance, 41–42
Flying snake, 36
Food, 13, 29, 30, 31, 32, 33, 34, 35–36,
  37, 41, 42, 43–51, 56, 57. *See also*
  Eating; Hunting
  snakes as, 62. *See also* Predators;
  Snake-eating snakes
Fox snake, 34, 59

Gaboon viper, *40*, 40, 48
Garter snake, *7*, 8, 34, 55, 57, 59, *61*
  common, 23, 34

San Francisco, *34*
Giant python, 54
Glands, 21, 48, 59
Gliding, 8, 19
Gopher snake, 34
Grass snake, 34
Green mamba, 38
Green snake, rough, *10*
Green tree python, 33, *53*
Growth, 55, 56

Habitats, 8, 32, 33, 34, 40, 41, 42, 62.
  See also Climate; Temperature
Head, *12*, 15, 19, 29, 35
Hearing, 8, 22–23. *See also* Ears
Heart, 9, 22
Heat, body, 9, 11, 13
Heat sensing, 25, 41
Hibernation, 56, 60
Hognose snake, 34, 53, *57*, 57–58
Hoods, 37–38, 57
Horned rattlesnake (sidewinder), 41, *42*
Hunting, 8, 21, 23–24, 25, 30, 35, 38, 41,
  43–51. *See also* Eating; Food
Hydrophiidae family, 28, 39

Indian python, *32*
Indian (spectacled) cobra, 37–38

Jacobson's organ, 24
Jaws, *12*, 20–21, 29, 37, 39, 41, 44, 47,
  50, 51
Joints, 14

Keel, 16
Keratin, 15
Kidneys, 22, 51
King brown snake, Australian, *37*, 37
King cobra, 37, 45, 53–54, 58
King snake, 34, *35*, 35–36, 45

Leg bones, 10, 11, 14, 26, 29
Legless lizards, *11*, 11, *12*
Leptotyphlopidae family, 28, 29
Lifespan, 56
Ligaments, 50
Litter size, 55
Liver, 22
Long-nosed whip snake, 23
Lungs, 8, 9, 22, 30, 41, 58
Lures, 45–46

Malaysian bronzeback, *43*
Male snakes, 52
Mamba, 28, 37, 38
  black, 38

common, 38
green, 38
Markings, 30, 31, 32, 34, 36, 38, 56, 59–60. *See also* Camouflage; Color
Mating, 24, 52–56
Mexican vine snake, 36
Milk snake, 36, 53, 57
Moccasin, 26, 29, 40
water (cottonmouth), 25, *29*, 29, 41, 59
Mojave rattlesnake, *22*
Movement, 6, 8, 11, 12, 14, 15, 18–19, 29, 35, 39, 41. *See also* Climbing
Muscles, 14, 18, 59

Names, Latin, 26, 28, 29
Neck/neck bones, 15, 45
Nests, 53–54
Night vision, 43
Noise (as defense), 58–59
Northern copperhead, *20*
Nostrils, 24

Organs, 14, 22–25

Panamint rattlesnake, *52*
Pelvic bones, 11, 14, 26, 29
Pine snake, 58
Pits, heat-sensitive, 25, 41
Pit vipers, 25, 39–40, 41–42
Poisonous snakes, 6, 21, 27, 35–36, 37–42, 45, 47–49, 56, 59–60. *See also* Venom
Prairie rattlesnake, *14*
Predators, 24–25, 36, 37, 38, 41, 56–60
Pregnancy, 55
Prey. *See* Eating; Food; Hunting
Puff adder, 40–41
Pupils, 23–24
Pygmy rattlesnake, 41
Python, 11, 15, 25, 28, 31, 33–34, 53
African, 6, 51
ball (royal), 33
giant, 54
green tree, 33, *53*
Indian, *32*
reticulated, 33
size of, 52

Racer, 34, 35
black, 53
Rat snake, *16*, 16, *26*, 34–35
everglades, *54*
yellow, *26*
Rattlesnake, 15, *25*, 25, 28, 39–40, 41, 43–44, 55, 59
eastern diamondback, *21*, 41

horned (sidewinder), 41, *42*
Mojave, *22*
panamint, *52*
prairie, *14*
pygmy, 41
timber, 23, *27*, 41
Rear-fanged snakes, 21, 36, 47
Regurgitation, 45, 46
Reproduction, 52–56
Reptiles, 9–10
Reticulated python, 33
Ribs, 14, 18, 19, 37, 49, 50
Rosy boa, 33, 55
Rough green snake, *10*
Rough-scaled viper, 58
Royal (ball) python, 33
Rubber boa, *33*, 33

Saliva/salivary glands, 49, 51
Scales, 8, 9, 10, *12*, 15–16, 29, 30, 41, 58, 59
Scutes, 15, 18. *See also* Scales
Sea snake, 19, 28, 39, 43
common, 39
yellow-bellied, 39
Senses, 8, 22–25
Shedding, of skin/tail, 17, 59
Shieldtail snake, 28, 30–31
Sidewinder (horned rattlesnake), 41, *42*
Sight, 22, 23–24
Skeleton, 9, 11, 14–15, 26
Skin, 9, 10, 11, *12*, 15–17, 37, 46, 59, 62
Skinks, 10
Skull, 14
Smell, 8, 22, 24–25, 34, 43, 48, 52, 59
Smooth snakes, 34
Snake-eating snakes, 30, 35–36, 37, 45, 57
Sounds, as defense, 58–59
Spectacled (Indian) cobra, 37–38
Spectacles, 16, 17
Sperm storage, 52–53
Spine (backbone), 14
Spines (on tail), 30
Spitting cobra, 38
Spraying, 59
Spurs, 11, 52
Sunbeam snake, 28, 30
Swallowing, 45, 47, 49–51
Swimming, 19

Tail, 15, 19, 29, 30–31, 33, 39, 41, 52, 59
Taipan, 37
Taste, 22, 24
Teeth, 21, 29, 31, 33, 44, 49, 51. *See also* Egg tooth

Temperature, 9, 11, 12, 25, 51, 55. *See also* Climate; Habitats
Texture, skin, 15–16
Thirst snake, 44
Thread snake, 28, 29
Tiger snake, 37
Timber rattlesnake, 23, *27*, 41
Tongue, 8, 24–25, 43, 45, 46
Touch, sense of, 25
Traps, 45–46
Tree boa, 19
emerald, 32, 33
Tree-climbing snakes, 19
Tree python, green, 33, *53*
Tree snakes, 15, *23*, 23, 24, 32, 33, 34, 36, 38, 43
Tuataras, 9
Typhlopidae family, 28, 29

Uropeltidae family, 28

Venom and venom glands, 21, 35–36, 38, 45, 48, 49, 56
Venomous snakes. *See* Poisonous snakes
Vertebrae, 14, 45, 59
Vertebrates, 22
Vibration, 22–23, 43, 58–59
Vine snake, *36*, 36
African, 45–46
Mexican, 36
Viper
blunt-nosed, 46
gaboon, *40*, 40, 48
pit, 25, 39–40, 41–42
rough-scaled, 58
Viperidae family, 15, 21, *27*, 28, 37–42, 39–42, 47–48, 49
Vision, 23–24. *See also* Eyes/eyesight

Warm-blooded animals, 11
Wart snake, 46
Wastes, 15, 51
Water moccasin (cottonmouth), 25, *29*, 29, 41, 59
Water snake, 34, 39
Whip snake, 35
long-nosed, *23*
Windpipe, 49, 58
Worm snake, 28, 29

Xenopeltidae family, 28, 30

Yellow-bellied sea snake, 39
Yellow rat snake, *26*
Yolk, 55